Neptune

The Ice Giant

Irma Bernabe

NEPTUNE

The Ice Giant

Irma Bernabe

Halo
PUBLISHING
INTERNATIONAL

Halo Publishing International
8000 W Interstate 10, #600
San Antonio, Texas 78230

First Edition, January 2023
Printed in the United States of America
ISBN: 978-1-63765-341-8

The information contained within this book is strictly for informational purposes. Unless otherwise indicated, all the names, characters, businesses, places, events and incidents in this book are either the product of the author's imagination or used in a fictitious manner. Any resemblance to actual persons, living or dead, or actual events is purely coincidental.

Halo Publishing International is a self-publishing company that publishes adult fiction and non-fiction, children's literature, self-help, spiritual, and faith-based books. We continually strive to help authors reach their publishing goals and provide many different services that help them do so. We do not publish books that are deemed to be politically, religiously, or socially disrespectful, or books that are sexually provocative, including erotica. Halo reserves the right to refuse publication of any manuscript if it is deemed not to be in line with our principles. Do you have a book idea you would like us to consider publishing? Please visit www.halopublishing.com for more information.

My first book, one of the many I hope, through God, will become a reality, I dedicate very especially to Nanas, who inspired me to write it, as well as to my dog Thalia and my cat Preciosa, my first daughters. They taught for the first time what it was to lose those special beings God places in our lives.

Here begins more than a short story, more than a text for entertainment; here begins the lives of various characters that bore witness to the story of an exceptional being, a being with a soul, spirit, great personality, and animal divinity.

All of us who love animals also respect them because they are souls that come to give us life lessons, and when they leave, they tear our hearts and leave a void on them, for we give them a very special place in our hearts and our families.

Neptune arrived at La Esperanza ranch. He was very far away from the city, where you could almost touch the moon and the immense sky full of stars. The ranch was next to the mountains, with different kinds of trees: pines, eucalyptus, and oaks. In that place, numerous wild animals lived, like bears, mountain lions, deers, wild cats, coyotes, squirrels, a great variety of birds, and one or two rabbits that looked for alfalfa in Neptune's feeder. At night, you could hear owls and crickets, which sang melodies that lulled the inhabitants of that place. Very far away, the lights and buildings of the city were visible.

Neptune's sight got lost between the distant lights as time passed, maybe thinking where Lucy was in that vast city. The ranch had animals, like chickens, roosters, which sang at early morning when the sun's radiance still didn't show up, a precious grey cat with white legs, and a mixed raced dog, a cross between a Pitbull and a German shepherd, with beautiful honey-colored eyes named Thalia, who always loved to chase the rabbits in Neptune's corral.

Lucy could not see Neptune at any of his races, which he won many times, nor could Neptune see Lucy at any of her famous concerts, but they did so always thinking of each other. Before walking up to the arena, as he did every time, he left everything on the racetrack, and Lucy played her superb violin on each stage. They both did it with their hearts and the hope of meeting again someday and never parting ways.

Lucy carried a medal that came to her heart; it had a gold coin with an engraved horse in the front and a note on the back that said: "A promise is never broken." This medal belonged to her grandmother, doña Regina Lomeli, and Lucy always kissed it before any of her concerts while thinking of Neptune. The memories came and went from the most beautiful moments they shared, and she always repeated in a low voice the promise she made to her grandma and Neptune: one day, she would look for him and get him back. Don Salvador Mendoza commissioned the medal for doña Regina; this was the present he would give her on their last Christmas together.

Don Salvador was a countryman dedicated to his family. He wore strap sandals, bell-bottom pants, and a navy-blue jacket, which highlighted his green eyes. His hair was hoary, had sideburns and a receding hairline that brought up his big personality. He wore a hat that never left his head; even though he had many to choose from, don Salvador always went out with the same one. Doña Regina constantly fought because of the blissful old hat that her husband wanted to carry everywhere. He was a good man, very religious, and with great customs and values. Every night, don Salvador drank pomegranate punch after coming home exhausted from working the field. He said it was for the fatigue and went out again to play with Ana, Lucy's mom. She asked him when they would buy her a horse of hers because the two horses they had were meant to plow the land. The poor horses ended up so tired that it would have been good to give them some punch for the fatigue as well.

In the town, the people whispered of that family having money, but they lived in precarious situations. They did not have any luxuries; their bespreads were made by doña Regina herself out of old cloth pieces that she cut into squares of different colors. They did not eat out, except for the churros bought after Sunday mass. They only got what was necessary from doña Juanita's shop: rice, flour, sugar, coffee, and cinnamon, which could not be missing in their household. Everything else they produced on their land, and with the three cows on their property, there always was fresh milk every morning and evening.

Doña Regina made cheese, "requeson," and with the cream, she baked some exquisite bread in tuna cans she kept every year during lent. She also had chickens that laid enough eggs for breakfast. All her chickens had their name and would call each to feed them; doña Regina knew them very well. Even though many were identical, she never confused them. She nagged them in the winter because they didn't lay more than two or three eggs per week. However, these eggs had golden yolks, five times more intense than their natural color and very thick; it was then when doña Regina took advantage of that to bake her tasty bread made of cream in a massive oven made of bricks, where Ana used to play and call it her home when it rained. The winter yolks were doña Regina's secret ingredient so her bread would come out with the best flavor and texture.

There was a huge avocado tree when you entered their home and a pomegranate tree right next to a stone sink, which don

Salvador employed in winter to make his famous punch for the rest of the year; he added guava, nuts, and green chili.

They planted corn, green beans, beans, onions, tomatoes, chilis, carrots, zucchini, potatoes, cilantro, and cucumbers in the garden. During the rainy season, wild purslanes would sprout yearly, which were doña Regina's favorite. She cooked like the archangels that sing in heaven, from refried beans, stuffed chilis, meatballs, green enchiladas, and sweet mole to her favorite dish: pork ribs with purslane, as well as prickly pear salad. And it was impossible to forget her desserts: "arroz con leche," honeyed sweet potato, plums with syrup, tamales with raisins, "capirotada" with cheese and raisins, which the town's priest loved, and vanilla flavored eggnog, that she also offered to her friends from church.

On Christmas night, don Salvador gifted the gold medal to doña Regina and made her promise that, if anything were to happen to him, they would leave for the USA, and as soon as they got there, she would buy a horse for Ana. Doña Regina said yes. Things were not good back then: the government was after the "cristeros", as they called them, and don Salvador was already one of them because he organized meetings and reunions and provided them with firearms along with the town's priest. They did all that to defend their faith and religious freedom; they were against the famous Calles law. The feds and agrarians were after them to shoot them.

One early morning they came; they went first for the town's priest. He was only twenty-one years. They shot and took him to the presidency to make an example out of him for those who rebelled. It was different with don Salvador and what doña Regina feared so much came true. The agrarians came for him and forced him out of his house in only his wild cotton underpants, with no sandals; they beat and tortured him so he would talk, but his silence only worsened the situation. With anger and abuse of power, they hung him by the avocado tree by his house's entrance. Doña Regina was prepared for such an atrocious event; many nights, she patched up her brown dress and wild cotton apron, which looked more like a skirt when worn over her dress. They filled all their bastilles with gold nuggets. That fateful night they lowered don Salvador from the tree. Doña Regina dressed him, placed his old hat on his head, the one he loved the most, wrapped him in a "zarape", and buried him under the avocado tree.

The early morning was nearing when doña Regina took Ana. She dressed her in a lime-colored dress, and they went far away due to the promise she made to don Salvador to look for a better future for their only daughter.

Doña Regina and Ana traveled to the city, leaving their town with pain and resignation, leaving don Salvador and the old house that used to be their lovely home.

The evening was getting closer when they arrived in California. They went to Father Emilio, who visited them often in their town. He was a close friend of the family. Doña Regina brought the address he shared in his many letters and postcards. She told him everything that happened with don Salvador while explaining there wasn't enough time to inform him before due to the tragic circumstances. He helped them and placed them happily in Martha's, his sister, house. While looking for a place for both, Father Emilio advised doña Regina to find a school for Ana. Money was no problem, so doña Regina bought a ranch and named it: Las Camelias ranch. Little by little, it would become a gorgeous ranch filled with white and pink camellias.

A neighbor brought Chester to doña Regina, a little black Chihuahua. Father Emilio arrived with two cats, one grey like the night called Simon, and the other was Whisky, colored white as cotton; he had an emerald-green eye, and the other was blue, like the sky. It wouldn't be long before Luna arrived at the ranch; she was the promise don Salvador made to Ana and which he assigned to doña Regina. A few days before Ana's seventh birthday, Luna arrived at Las Camelias. She was a white Arab horse colored like clouds; she had big charcoal-bordered black eyes as if they were traced on purpose. Luna came to fill Ana's void due to changing countries and languages, and above all, due to losing her father.

School was tough; at the beginning, it wasn't easy, but little by little, with the help of Father Emilio and Martha, Ana and doña Regina got accustomed to their new little town and Father Emilio's church.

Ana and Luna spent a lot of time together. Ana loved drawing Luna and did nothing but talk about her at school. One day, her teacher asked to meet with doña Regina to discuss how all of Ana's schoolwork spoke only about Luna. The teacher told doña Regina that she needed to explain to Ana that her world didn't revolve around Luna and that her work could be related to different subjects, but it was impossible. Ana was stubborn and kept writing short stories about Luna as if those were their diaries. Finally, the teacher gave up while reading Ana and Luna's daily compositions.

Doña Regina never married again; she devoted herself to raising her only child. She sent Ana to the best schools with Father Emilio's help, and in less than a year, Ana spoke her second language perfectly.

Time went by incredibly fast; Ana was about to turn fifteen. She became a beautiful lady with fair skin, black hair like velvet, and big brown eyes, like her mother's. She and her mother planned a celebration with Father

Emilio, Martha, her boyfriend Luis, and Blanca, Ana's only friend. They went out, and due to all their chatter, they got home very late to a displeasing surprise: a coyote had attacked Chester and was agonizing because of the terrible bites on his neck. Ana ran and took him into her arms. Moments later, Chester passed away. It was as if he was only waiting to say goodbye. Doña Regina and Ana cried heavily; with tears in their eyes, they dug a hole in the garden to bury Chester. Doña Regina wrapped him in a shawl she was wearing that night; it was very colorful and had a peacock print. They buried him with his favorite toys, among them a slipper that belonged to Ana when she was younger. They filled the grave with white camellias.

Another day, Martha arrived in the morning and let out some horrific screams that woke Ana and her mother. They went down immediately, and, as it turns out, some coyotes had smelled Chester's corpse and dragged it out while eating his legs. Doña Regina told

Martha to please take Ana away while Luis arrived to bury Chester again. Luis placed him into a box filled with lime and put it in a much deeper hole where the coyotes couldn't dig him out again. That was poor Chester's tragic fate.

Three years later, the day for Ana to leave her mother arrived. She had a scholarship at one of the best universities. Ana would attend veterinary school due to growing up around animals from a young age. One of doña Regina's favorite anecdotes was of Ana when she was little; her chicken Vilma was her first patient and died while putting an egg. Ana didn't like her mother telling that story, which motivated her to become one of the best veterinarians one day.

Ana met Peter, Lucy's father, at her university. He was white, thin tall and came from a good family. He studied psychology. They hadn't finished school when the army started drafting people. Peter and his brother were forced to defend their country, but before he left, Peter decided to marry Ana. He proposed to her on Ana's birthday and gave her an engagement ring that belonged to his mother; it was shaped like the sun and had engraved diamonds.

Doña Regina prepared a small banquet for Ana and Peter with their friends and Peter's family. She decorated Las Camelias with white "papel picado" with doves and hearts; some even said: "Ana and Peter." There were many flowers, among them roses, carnations, dahlias, and hydrangeas, all of which were white and eucalyptus branches. The event was out in the open in Las Camelias.

Doña Regina spent all night cooking pork "adobo," refried beans, white rice with vegetables, salads, and what could not be missing from the wedding: her delicious eggnog. She also prepared "cafe de olla" with loads of cinnamon and many desserts with fruits, sugar, and liqueur.

The ceremony was very intimate but in good taste. Father Emilio married Peter and Ana with tears in his eyes, for he had been like a second father to Ana, and the memories of her when she first arrived in this country as a little, chatty, filled with ideas-child came flooding. Now he saw her as a woman dressed in white on the altar.

The day came when Peter had to bid farewell to the love of his life. He promised they would never be separated again when the war ended, and they would have five children and many animals. Little did they know about the cruel fate that waited for them.

Ana wrote to Peter daily; she told him the good and bad news. After nine months, a letter arrived for Peter informing him that he had fathered a beautiful daughter that looked like him. Doña Regina was thrilled and called the child Lucy. Peter fell in love with his daughter when he saw how gorgeous she was, although he only got three more pictures of Lucy so he could see how Lucy was growing up.

One early morning, the doorbell at Las Camelias rang. Ana and doña Regina got up scared and thought about who it could be at that hour. That day everything went upside down. Peter had died in combat, and two officers were at the door to give them the terrible news. Ana fainted. When she got a hold of herself, Ana called Peter's parents, who arrived at Las Camelias at night. The funeral was heartbreaking for Ana and Peter's parents.

Doña Regina and Martha took care of Lucy while Ana mourned. She had to move on after losing Peter. The love of her life left her alone with Lucy, who carried their dreams, hopes, futures, and all the promises they had made to each other. In between crying and despair, Ana shouted without explanation, and no answer would give her peace and comfort; only sadness, pain, and uncertainty enveloped her even more in her tragedy. So went the days and the weeks.

Lucy woke up one morning and said her first word: "Ma-ma... ma-ma." That's when Ana responded and understood she had a lot to live for and move forward: she had her mother, who loved her deeply; she had Peter's parents, who supported her and gave her strength; and, above all, she had Lucy, a piece that Peter had left for Ana, living proof of their great love, like a shooting star. That was more than enough to turn the page. Ana had gone through her mourning period and no longer had any tears. Now was the time to fight, confront life, and be thankful. Besides, she had Father Emilio, who comforted her and showed her fortitude. Ana would always be on his mother and daughter's side, so she went back to school to finish the dream she and Peter had.

It was already spring, and chaos reigned in Las Camelias: there was a huge party.

Lucy was turning five, and Ana graduated from veterinary school after many sacrifices. Doña Regina took care of the cooking and the flowers, as she always did. Everything was perfect and delicious. Ana gifted her diploma to Lucy as a birthday present; it was thanks to her that Ana kept fighting after Peter's death. They shared an embrace, and Lucy placed a pink camellia on her mother's beautiful black hair, which reached her waist and highlighted the wine-colored dress she wore on that special occasion.

Ana started working at an emergency hospital. Don Raul, a friend of Father Emilio, wasn't mistaken in giving her the opportunity she dearly desired. Ana tended to the animals of her small town and was very professional, but, above all, she loved and respected each of her patients.

One day, Ana got home with a German Shepperd puppy. Lucy called him Rocco. Besides being intelligent, Rocco was very naughty and playful: he bit Lucy's shoes and tore down the clothes that Martha hung up; only screams could be heard when Martha had to pick up the clothes from the ground.

Summer was about to begin; Lucy's favorite days were arriving. She and her mother went out to lie down on the roof of their house. Ana told Lucy that they were like two lizards sunbathing. They meditated in the morning or the afternoon after Ana got home from work. She played with Lucy and her dolls, drank tea, and played cards and lottery with doña Regina at night. They were also accompanied by Martha and Luis, who worked with them, and now and then, Father Emilio would join as well. On Sundays, doña Regina, Lucy, and Ana went to church. After mass, they bought donuts. Ana thought about his father and told Lucy about their stories together.

During January, in the middle of the winter, one night, Luna was sick with colic due to the low temperatures. Everyone stayed with her until the early morning: Ana, Lucy, doña Regina, Martha, Luis, and even Father Emilio. Accompanied by some hot chocolate and pineapple "tamales," Ana walked Luna from side to side and gave her tempered water to see if the colic had gone; however, Luna only worsened. Ana cleansed Luna's stomach with oil and gave her a shot for the pain. Luna only wallowed. Her sweat was ice-cold, and her breathing became agitated. Ana had no choice but to euthanize Luna; her heart was aching. Ana took out two syringes: one was to relax Luna, and the other was to end her suffering. With tears in her eyes and rubbing Luna's neck with cotton, Ana injected the tranquilizer while everyone got closer so they could caress Luna. Everyone thanked her for all she had brought to Las Camelias: peace, tranquility, comfort, joy, and unconditional love. Ana grabbed the second syringe; her hands were shaking, and she didn't know if it was due to the cold, fear, or guilt of what she was about to do. Little by little, Ana administered the substance that would take away Luna's suffering forever. She covered Luna's face with a mustard-colored handkerchief, and the horse breathed for the last time. Ana whispered a prayer in Luna's ear, checked for a pulse, and lay down on her while screaming with pain and guilt. Luna's suffering had stopped. Lucy fell asleep in Martha's arms but was woken by her mother's screams. Lucy was very young and couldn't understand what was happening; she only cuddled next to her mother and Luna and showered Ana with kisses so she would feel better. Rocco wouldn't stop howling, as if he felt Luna's death.

Father Emilio helped to cover Luna with a thick blanket while the sun came up; if they left her uncovered, the coyotes would also eat her and die.

Ana caught a cold some days before Luna died, and that early morning she went into the house with a horrible fever. A few hours were left until sunrise, and doña Regina immediately called Dr. Alvarez so he would check on Ana, who didn't look very well.

Days and nights went by, and doña Regina and Martha took care of Ana with medicine, warm tea, and a good diet; however, no matter how hard they tried, it was already too late. Anna had pneumonia and was dying. Another loss, another tragedy, another sorrow for doña Regina. Father Emilio didn't leave them alone at any point; he was there like he always was for Ana's birthdays, graduations, and antics, and now he was there for her deathbed.

Dr. Alvarez left the room and left Lucy and doña Regina with Ana, one on each side of the oak bed where Ana rested. Lucy took shelter in her mother's arms and showered her with kisses; she told Ana that when she got better, they would buy another horse, go up to the roof and sunbathe like lizards, and buy donuts after mass. Lucy couldn't find a way to cheer up her mother. Ana asked her mother to take care of Lucy, and doña Regina told her she would do everything Lucy asked.

That night it began to rain. Unaware that the rain would take away Ana's last breath, doña Regina left to call Father Emilio and Martha. Lucy didn't want to let go of her mother, and they had to separate them by force. Martha left the room with Lucy in her arms, went down the stairs, gave her an umbrella, put her red boots with white polka dots on Lucy, and took her to the garden to pick up some camellias for Ana.

Dr. Alvarez and Father Emilio took care of Ana and her funeral. Meanwhile, doña Regina was cooking like crazy, maybe to ease the pain and impotence of not being able to help her daughter. She thought of how Lucy, being so small, was orphaned. Now it was only the two of them. While grilling some peppers, doña Regina threshed pomegranates and peeled nuts; the memories of her daughter overwhelmed her, and tears flowed along her sharp and perfect face. She cooked all night.

People started to arrive at Las Camelias as the word spread about Ana through the small town. The townspeople loved Ana.

Father Emilio couldn't officiate the funeral mass, so he called another priest from another parish. He was heartbroken and was not able to stand on his feet. Doña Regina cheered him up and gave him the strength needed, for she saw a tall and well-built man fall upon God's plan. Father Emilio questioned, shouting and filled with pain and rage, confronted and challenged God, asking why He took away Ana, who still had a life ahead of her and a daughter to raise. However, he didn't get a clear answer until doña Regina slapped him hard to calm him down; she made him see it was God's right to give and take life from whoever He pleases, and if taking Ana was his will, then they only needed to be humble.

All that was left was to respect and accept the loss of Ana. Father Emilio got on his knees and asked God's forgiveness for everything he said while sad and in pain. He got up, leaning on Ana's coffin, and said: "Everything will be fine. We will face this instead of Lucy."

The funeral was sorrowful. At the church, beautiful things were said about Ana, about the short time she worked at the hospital and how she asked the families of hopeless animals to thank them for all they had done in their lives. She then euthanized them and covered their faces with the handkerchiefs doña Regina sowed with pretty embroidery of multiple colors; she always whispered a prayer for them as if it were a rite for the souls of each of her patients.

After the funeral, Peter's parents decided to take Lucy away from Las Camelias for a few days; it would distract her a little.

For Lucy, the days were magical when she heard the music her grandfather played on the piano while she and her grandmother ate chocolate ice cream. One day, they went out to eat and then to a music store; her grandfather said, "Think about which instrument you would like to play." There was all kind of instruments at the shop, but Lucy threw herself without thinking towards a white violin with black strings. Her grandfather was surprised and said: "Are you sure about your choice?" In response, Lucy jumped up and down, saying yes with her index finger and showing an angel-like smile. Lucy told her grandparents she would play beautiful songs for her parents to hear in heaven.

Lucy was a very smart, strong, and mature child because of what life had thrown at her. Aside from being beautiful, she looked a lot like Ana, but her hair was clear as honey and her eyes blue, like Peter's.

Spring was nearing. Lucy arrived at Las Camelias with a ruckus; she was saying so many things to doña Regina, who she hadn't seen in weeks, that it was impossible to understand her.

Doña Regina had a good attitude in the face of Ana's death. She cried as she did for don Salvador, but now it was time to smile and see a new beginning and life for Lucy and her without their dear Ana. Unwavering faith comforted doña Regina, who had no self-pity for her loss and situation; she was a living example of fortitude for Lucy. "That kind of event we must always await during our lives; death is at the corner for everyone, and we must not fear it," doña Regina said.

When Lucy asked where her mother was, doña Regina told her she was flying as a butterfly among all the camellias in the garden and that Ana would always be with them. The days passed, and Lucy ran to her violin every time she saw a butterfly flying; the sounds made were atrocious, and even the strings broke as she said: "Mommy, I will play a song for you with my violin."

Every morning, Lucy would kiss a picture of her parents that sat by the house's entrance, next to a flower vase filled with camellias she and doña Regina placed before leaving for mass. Lucy would also say goodbye to her parents whenever she stepped through the door, whether it was to leave for school, go to church or leave for a trip to visit her grand-parents on her father's side.

When Lucy turned nine, don Raul arrived at Las Camelias with a huge surprise; it was a gift arranged by doña Regina: Condesa, a white mare filled with freckles all over her body. And that wasn't it. Condesa was preg-nant, something Lucy couldn't believe. She was over the moon and couldn't stop talking because of her immense joy. Doña Regina only looked at Lucy and smiled due to seeing her happy.

Winter came; it was one of the harshest there had been and ever would be. It was early morning when doña Regina wandered from side to side. The sun hadn't come up when don Raul got out of the stable and said: "It was a difficult birth; Condesa is gone. I did everything possible to save both, but I had to choose one." A big, beautiful, white-as-now foal was born. He was quickly covered in a wool blanket to protect him from the cold.

Lucy showed up, skipping joyfully, and telling doña Regina if the new horse was already here and if it was a boy or a girl, for she had chosen a name for it a long time ago; doña Regina told her: "Go and look at him. He is a foal, but his mother went with yours." Lucy's face changed instantly; she went to the tiny foal and told him: "Now there's two of us, but don't worry, grandma will also be your mom. She will take good care of us; you'll see." Lucy hugged Condesa and thanked her: "Thank you for your baby; thank you for leaving him with us." Like

Ana, Lucy covered Condesa's face, told her she would care for him, whispered a prayer in her ear, and gently hugged the foal. Doña Regina, to comfort her granddaughter, asked: "And what is the name you have for him?" "His name will be Neptune, like the planet," Lucy responded. That's how Lucy named the small creature.

Lucy and Martha spent long hours feeding Neptune. Lucy played her violin, which the horse enjoyed profoundly, and their days and months went by. Between Lucy and Neptune, it was already visible that their energy flowed at the same level; they also shared many things in common: they didn't have parents, shared the same mother, and loved music.

Lucy and Martha always cared for the young horse; they played with Rocco and Neptune. Meanwhile, doña Regina did her chores, like looking out for the house and taking Lucy to school and back home; she also helped Father Emilio by doing whatever was needed at his church. And when night came, doña Regina would help Lucy with her homework, play lottery, pray for their loved ones, and warm up some milk with honey and cinnamon to help her granddaughter sleep.

It was a Sunday; Lucy and doña Regina were returning from mass at noon. Doña Regina felt ill: she was short of breath and held her chest. Lucy threw her donut on the sidewalk to help her grandma stand up. She carefully took her grandma home, with the help of Luis and Martha, who were nearby, and heard Lucy's cry for help. They called Dr. Alvarez to check up on the older woman. There was no good news.

Doña Regina had a bad heart, and it seemed as if her days were numbered. So, before tragedy struck, she called Father Emilio to help her take care of everything, leaving Lucy and Neptune in good hands. Doña Regina told Luis to speak with don Ramiro Ruelas, owner of Golden sun estate, so that he would look at Neptune; to their surprise, when he saw the horse, he said: "I'll take him. I will send for him tomorrow at sunrise." Don Ramiro paid significant money because he knew Neptune's real value.

That night, doña Regina bid farewell to Neptune. "Always remember, Neptune, you are an exceptional being. Your abilities go way beyond those of an ordinary horse, so take advantage of them and never give up on life because you will always find love on your path," she repeated to the horse. Lucy heard the same thing from her grandma, and the older woman made her promise that one day, she would get Neptune back to care for him and be by his side until the end.

Lucy played her violin all night to say goodbye to Neptune. Martha made her company until the following day when Neptune would go away. That's how Neptune lost his second mother and Lucy, who ran after him, shouting, while he was taken away in don

Ramiro's elegant trailer. That same day, doña Regina took Lucy to Peter's parents, and a few days later, she took another trip, never to see her loved ones again.

Father Emilio, Martha, and Luis arranged doña Regina's funeral, who left everything ready for her service, from the coffin to her clothes and mass. Doña Regina didn't wish for Lucy to see her in agony, so she decided to take her to Peter's parents before everything happened. They buried the older woman next to her beloved Ana, as she wanted.

That's how Neptune left Las Camelias ranch and arrived at Golden sun estate. He thought he would find people filled with love at his new home, like doña Regina and Lucy; however, it was the opposite. Don Ramiro was a cold person whose only wish was to become even more prosperous. Nonetheless, that didn't matter to Neptune, who took part in every training imposed on him, always thinking that he would find love again in his life journey like doña Regina said the day he left Las Camelias. So went by the days and the months.

Neptune started to compete and win in his first races; his name and fame grew fast. He was constantly surrounded by photographers, trainers, and fans, always with awards, compliments, and attention. However, the horse was locked up after every race, and he felt lonelier than ever.

Lucy kept growing, and her paternal grandparents put the young woman in a school where her violin skills improved daily; she quickly became one of the school's best players. Lucy thought it wouldn't be long before she could look for Neptune.

The days passed as fast as the news, and everyone was getting ready for the big event. Neptune had risen like the tide, and he stood as the ice giant he was, for he would compete in one last race before going directly to the Kentucky Derby, where only a few can race, only the most outstanding and notable horses, like Neptune.

Everyone was anxious at the arena. The beasts charged against the doors, yearning for freedom. The newscasters waited for what was about to unfold in that place. The fanfare began, and the horse's gates opened. Neptune got out at full throttle, as he used to. Carlos, his rider, gave him a lot of confidence; he carried an elegant turquoise suit with a sun embroidered on the back. He and Neptune stood out among all the participants.

Neptune battered all his opponents. The race was ending, and the sand cut by the legs of every horse as if they were swords. Don Ramiro was already celebrating his triumph, he imagined himself counting his money and toasting at the Kentucky Derby, but that didn't happen. Neptune took a wrong step on the sand, which was wet due to the recent rains, and fell like an ice giant. Everything became silent and was recorded before the eyes of hundreds of spectators. That would be Neptune's last race, who unconsciously heard a far-away voice that said: "Neptune, never give up; remember that your path in life will make you find love and happiness again."

The mighty horse woke up and felt unbearable pain in his back leg, which had a big bandage. He tried to get up, but his leg couldn't hold such a corpulent figure.

Don Ramiro Ruelas was furious because Neptune lost the race just seconds away from getting to the finish line, and above all, because of the amount of money he lost gambling; that mattered more to him than the well-being of Neptune.

Despite Neptune's great fall, Carlos never left his side and said to him: "Don't worry, my giant. Everything will be fine, I promise you. I won't let anyone hurt you; like the rest of the animals that pass through here."

Don Ramiro went to Neptune's veterinarian, who told him the tragic news: Neptune would never step on a racetrack again; he had to be put down. The estate owner's fury was so great that he took out his revolver and pointed it toward Neptune's head. However, Carlos took the gun away from don Ramiro and told him: "Go to rest, don Ramiro. I will take care of him." As don Ramiro was walking away, Carlos raised the gun, and a gunshot was heard.

Carlos's intent was different from don Ramiro's. He and Neptune traveled together while the latter was sedated entirely with analgesics. Carlos drove for several hours, thinking Neptune deserved another chance and this wasn't his final destination.

At last, Carlos arrived at La Esperanza ranch. The rider went to his brother Javier to tell him he had an exceptional gift for him and hoped he would gladly accept it because it would need much care and attention.

Things were not good for Javier. He and his wife, Eva, were going through difficult times; they were mournful due to losing their child, who was supposed to be born around that time.

Javier and Eva walked with curiosity toward the trailer that carried Neptune, and when they opened the doors, they were bewitched by the horse's immense beauty and size. They carefully took Neptune to the barn, which only had three sacks of hen food.

Eva and Javier started to care for Neptune; day and night, they would stay awake, but the horse wouldn't get better; he lost his appetite, especially the will to live and move forward.

One morning, Javier arrived with a gift for Eva because of her birthday. She was trying to feed Neptune, but it was always useless. Javier hugged and kissed her, saying: "Happy birthday, dear." He gave Eva a box that had a giant pink bow. She anxiously broke the wrapping paper. "A radio," she said with enthusiasm. Eva placed the radio on a table, switched it on, and put on a station that played a pretty melody. It was Lucy. Neptune neighed and pricked up his ears; the tune was familiar to him. Soon, the horse went through his memories and remembered that the melody was the song that Lucy used to play for him when she was a child. That song was special to him, so, as he could, Neptune got up and started to take small bites from the grain that Eva had prepared minutes earlier. Eva began to weep and told the horse: "Neptune, this is the best birthday present you could have given me." She got close to the stallion and kissed him on the head. That's how the ice giant's recovery began.

Eva turned on the radio daily for Neptune, and Lucy's songs would still be playing on the same station. Eva couldn't imagine what it meant for the ice giant to hear the violinist, but to him, that was the best medicine for his recovery and to motivate him. Not only did Neptune come back to life, but he was also reborn. Hope came once more; the stallion knew he would find love and happiness in his journey like doña Regina always talked about.

Each day, Neptune was delighted by Lucy's music. He no longer walked; he galloped. It even seemed as if he was flying. Eva and Javier were surprised by Neptune's recovery, but even more so about that violinist's music healing him; it was like a miracle.

Lucy finally arrived at Las Camelias. Father Emilio, Martha, Luis, and her friend Blanca eagerly waited for her, and they told her the news: the coyotes had eaten Simon, the cat. Dr. Alvarez took in Rocco, and Whisky was with Father Emilio at the church's house. Martha prepared Lucy's favorite meal: refried beans, green "chilaquiles," and "cecina." Lucy wept while remembering her mother and grandmother. After eating, everyone went to the cemetery to place some camellias for Ana and doña Regina. Lucy talked about going to see don Ramiro to get Neptune back; everything would be like when his grandmother was alive. She offered Martha and Luis the chance to return and work at the ranch, but she never imagined what would happen afterward.

The next morning, Lucy arrived at Golden sun estate, which took don Raul by surprise. He told her about the fame and fortune made thanks to Neptune and that a fatal accident ended his career during his last race, so they had to put him down. Lucy couldn't hold back and threw herself over with fury, screaming to don Raul that he was a petty, heartless, and reprehensible person. How could they do that to Neptune? How did he end the life of such a beautiful being? Lucy returned to Las Camelias with a shattered heart, still weeping for Neptune.

The following morning, Lucy said goodbye to Martha and Luis; then, she left for a tour that would last for months. Lucy continuously poured all her pain into her melodies, dedicating them to her loved ones, especially Neptune. She couldn't keep the promise to the horse or her grandma about staying by the ice giant's side until the end. However, Neptune's physical, mental and spiritual health completely recovered at La Esperanza. Lucy never imagined that her music was the best medicine for Neptune's recovery, even less that he was still alive.

Little by little, Eva started to ride Neptune. He would let himself be loved and pampered by her and Javier; they loved Neptune like the son they never got to hold in their arms. The horse brought joy and fullness to their lives. Neptune had finally encountered the love and happiness that doña Regina talked about; now, he had two special people that loved him without conditions and conveniences; he found parents in his life's path and was now a part of a small family.

Eva and Neptune became inseparable. They went out to ride, and Thalia, the dog, would always tag along. That's how the years passed.

Eva would turn on the old radio every afternoon, which still played Lucy's melodies. Meanwhile, she would bathe Neptune. On the other hand, Javier showered them with gifts daily: carrots, apples, and molasses for Neptune; gemstones, feathers, and wildflowers he found along the road for Eva.

Meanwhile, Lucy was still on tour worldwide, trying to forget his life and the one she imagined having when she returned home. She visited her grandparents and Blanca and later spent a few days at Las Camelias with Martha, Luis, and their two children.

One day, while Eva was riding Neptune, he began to limp with the same leg injured years ago during his last race. With a lot of difficulties, they returned to La Esperanza. Eva quickly called Neptune's veterinarian; the receptionist told her that Dr. Bernabe wasn't in town but that another veterinarian oversaw the clinic during his absence. Eva told the receptionist it was an emergency and urgently needed the veterinarian to visit La Esperanza ranch.

The veterinarian arrived at the ranch very fast, and it happened to be don Raul. To his immense surprise, after more than fifteen years, Neptune was still as beautiful as when he took care of Condesa's labor. Above all, don Raul was surprised to find him many years later, far from when he was born. Immediately, don Raul asked how Neptune got there; he then proceeded to tell Eva and Javier who Neptune's mother was and the sad circumstances under which he was separated from doña Regina and Lucy. Eva and

Javier were shocked by Neptune's story as told by don Raul, for it seemed that he was talking about a very different horse. After checking up on Neptune and still without a precise diagnosis, don Raul ordered some studies to discard what his eyes were seeing on Neptune's leg.

The following morning, don Raul arrived with tragic news for Eva and Javier. Neptune's fall had dire consequences as time passed: the horse's right leg had developed terminal cancer. There was nothing to be done, not even amputating the leg; there was only one thing left: put him down, for he was suffering due to the horrible pain the disease was starting to cause.

Neptune's health worsened daily; he was no longer able to walk, and little by little, he stopped eating. Regardless of the care they gave to the ice giant, Javier and Eva knew that he wouldn't get better, so they would have to make a tragic choice as soon as possible to avoid further suffering for Neptune.

Carlos arrived at La Esperanza after he found out what was happening to accompany Javier and Eva. There was no way he could save Neptune again, but he was happy that Neptune had a life that any horse would have wished for many years.

Don Raul went looking for Lucy to inform her that Neptune was alive but agonizing and that she had to say goodbye to him. She couldn't believe what don Raul claimed; it was like a miracle fading away. Lucy thought she didn't have time to waste and how it was that Neptune still lived after all those years.

Lucy quickly got out of her changing room, leaving a stage filled with people eagerly waiting to hear her play. She only took her violin. Lucy entered don Raul's car once she exited the luxurious venue. The violinist immediately called Martha and Luis, who called Father Emilio, so they would all meet at La Esperanza.

Neptune was agonizing in the barn next to Eva and Javier. Suddenly, Lucy's melody was heard. Neptune straightened his long, furry neck with tremendous effort to look at the old radio that played the tune. It wasn't the radio; Lucy was by his side, weeping while playing her violin. The memories were spinning inside Lucy's head; she thought fate had cruelly separated them, brought them back together, and now it was offering the last chance to fulfill a promise. Slowly, the ice giant melted into the magical melody that Lucy played with her violin.

Don Raul raised his hand to signal to Javier and Eva that it was time to say goodbye to Neptune and thank him for the unconditional love and happiness he brought to their lives. Martha, Luis, and Father Emilio were also there.

Lucy removed her kerchief with patterned butterflies from her neck and covered Neptune's face. She whispered a short prayer in his ear as her mother showed her: "Fly high for love, respect, and dignity; let the universe claim you. Thank you for your life, your teachings, and the happiness you brought into my life." And so, Neptune's life went away with the wind and Lucy's melody.

I met Neptune; he was an extraordinary being to whom I dedicate this story in his honor about his beginning and end. I also dedicate it to the giants like him who were sacrificed for cruel races, all for money and ambition.

I also want to dedicate this book to Eva and Javier, whose hearts were shattered by losing their second son.

Neptune's friends, including me, were there for his last moments and cried for him. His memories will forever remain in the hearts of those who knew him and truly loved him unconditionally.

Through the years, Eva and Javier continued to decorate, with flowers, photographs, and his long white braid, the trunk where they keep the ashes of what once was: Neptune, the ice giant.

In life, there will always be losses, maybe of a loved one, a house, a job, or a friendship, but never forget that a life journey is long; just give it a chance, and there you will find love again in a very different way. You only need hope and faith that a good day will come; meanwhile, enjoy the journey.

The past is gone, and the future doesn't exist; love, live, and enjoy the present.